Ben, Billy, and the Birdhouse

The Sound of B

by Cecilia Minden and Joanne Meier • illustrated by Bob Ostrom

The Child's World

Published by The Child's World®
1980 Lookout Drive
Mankato, MN 56003-1705
800-599-READ
www.childsworld.com

The Child's World®: Mary Berendes, Publishing Director
The Design Lab: Design and page production

Library of Congress Cataloging-in-Publication Data
 Minden, Cecilia.
  Ben, Billy, and the birdhouse : the sound of B /
by Cecilia Minden and Joanne Meier ; illustrated
by Bob Ostrom.
     p. cm.
  ISBN 978-1-60253-394-3 (library bound : alk. paper)
  1. English language—Consonants—Juvenile literature.
2. English language—Phonetics—Juvenile literature 3.
Reading—Phonetic method—Juvenile literature. I. Meier,
Joanne D. II. Ostrom, Bob,
 ill. III. Title.
  PE1159.M4525 2010
  [E]—dc22   2010013395

Printed in the United States of America in Mankato, MN.
July 2010
F11538

NOTE TO PARENTS AND EDUCATORS:

The Child's World® has created this series with the goal of exposing children to engaging stories and illustrations that assist in phonics development. The books in the series will help children learn the relationships between the letters of written language and the individual sounds of spoken language. This contact helps children learn to use these relationships to read and write words.

The books in this series follow a similar format. An introductory page, to be read by an adult, introduces the child to the phonics feature, or sound, that will be highlighted in the book. Read this page to the child, stressing the phonic feature. Help the student learn how to form the sound with her mouth. The story and engaging illustrations follow the introduction. At the end of the story, word lists categorize the feature words into their phonic elements.

Each book in this series has been carefully written to meet specific readability requirements. Close attention has been paid to elements such as word count, sentence length, and vocabulary. Readability formulas measure the ease with which the text can be read and understood. Each book in this series has been analyzed using the Spache readability formula.

Reading research suggests that systematic phonics instruction can greatly improve students' word recognition, spelling, and comprehension skills. This series assists in the teaching of phonics by providing students with important opportunities to apply their knowledge of phonics as they read words, sentences, and text.

This is the letter b.

In this book, you will read words
that have the **b** sound as in:
bird, box, bag, and *ball.*

I am Ben.

This is my best friend, Billy.

Billy is also my brother!

This is our Uncle Bob.
We are building a house
for a bird.

8

Here is a box of wood.

We will need wood.

Here is a bag of nails.

We will need nails.

Uncle Bob cuts the wood.

The boys build the house.

It is a beautiful house.

They paint it bright blue.

Uncle Bob finds a branch.

He hangs up the house.

"Someday I will build houses. The houses will be big," says Ben.

"Someday I will build parks. Children can play ball," says Billy.

"Look," says Uncle Bob.

"A bird is in the house!"

Fun Facts

Not all birds will make their nests in birdhouses. Owls, woodpeckers, chickadees, wrens, bluebirds, starlings, martins, sparrows, and finches are some that do. Other birds, however, prefer to live in groups. As a result, some people build birdhouses that resemble miniature apartment buildings. These birdhouses have more than one level and can house more than 20 birds!

If you like building things, imagine helping build the Petronas Twin Towers in Malaysia. Many people consider this to be the tallest building in the world! Willis Tower in Chicago, Illinois, is the tallest building in the United States.

Activity

Building Your Own Birdhouse
With the help of a parent or other adult, you can build your own birdhouse! First, decide what kind of bird you are building the house for. This will affect the size and shape of the house, as well as the materials you use to build it. Once you have finished the birdhouse, pick a good place to put your birdhouse. Many people say the best spot is near a tree or bush. Once the birdhouse is built, keep a journal describing the bird or birds that move in.

To Learn More

Books
About the Sound of B
Moncure, Jane Belk. *My "b" Sound Box®*. Mankato, MN: The Child's World, 2009.

About Best Friends
Kellogg, Steven. *Best Friends*. New York: Dial Books for Young Readers, 1986.

Marshall, James. *George and Martha: The Complete Stories of Two Best Friends*. Boston: Houghton Mifflin, 2008.

About Birdhouses
Wellington, Monica. *Riki's Birdhouse*. New York: Dutton Children's Books, 2009.

Ziefert, Harriet, and Donald Dreifuss (illustrator). *Birdhouse for Rent*. Boston: Houghton Mifflin, 2001.

About Building Things
Johnson, D. B. *Henry Builds a Cabin*. Boston: Houghton Mifflin, 2002.

Luxbacher, Irene. *123 I Can Build!* Toronto: Kids Can Press, 2009.

Web Sites
Visit our home page for lots of links about the Sound of B:

childsworld.com/links

Note to Parents, Teachers, and Librarians: We routinely check our Web links to make sure they're safe, active sites—so encourage your readers to check them out!

B Feature Words

Proper Names

Ben

Billy

Bob

Feature Words in Initial Position

bag

ball

beautiful

best

big

bird

box

boy

build

building

Feature Words with Blends

blue

branch

bright

brother

About the Authors

Cecilia Minden, PhD, is the former director of the Language and Literacy Program at the Harvard Graduate School of Education. She is now a reading consultant for school and library publications. She earned her PhD in reading education from the University of Virginia. Cecilia and her husband, Dave Cupp, live outside Chapel Hill, North Carolina. They enjoy sharing their love of reading with their grandchildren, Chelsea and Qadir.

Joanne Meier, PhD, has worked as an elementary school teacher, university professor, and researcher. She earned her BA in early childhood education from the University of South Carolina, and her MEd and PhD in education from the University of Virginia. She currently works as a literacy consultant for schools and private organizations. Joanne lives in Virginia with her husband Eric, daughters Kella and Erin, two cats, and a gerbil.

About the Illustrator

Bob Ostrom has been illustrating children's books for nearly twenty years. A graduate of the New England School of Art & Design at Suffolk University, Bob has worked for such companies as Disney, Nickelodeon, and Cartoon Network. He lives in North Carolina with his wife Melissa and three children, Will, Charlie, and Mae.